CLEVER CUB

and the Easter Surprise

Bob Hartman

Illustrated by Steve Brown

DAVID C COOK

transforming lives together

CLEVER CUB AND THE EASTER SURPRISE
Published by David C Cook
4050 Lee Vance Drive
Colorado Springs, CO 80918 U.S.A.

Integrity Music Limited, a Division of David C Cook
Brighton, East Sussex BN1 2RE, England

The graphic circle C logo is a registered trademark of David C Cook.

All Scripture paraphrases are based on the ESV® Bible (The Holy Bible, English Standard Version®),
copyright © 2001 by Crossway, a publishing ministry of Good News Publishers.
Used by permission. All rights reserved.

Library of Congress Control Number 2021936130
ISBN 978-0-8307-8254-3

© 2021 Bob Hartman
Illustrations by Steve Brown. Copyright © 2021 David C Cook

The Team: Laura Derico, Stephanie Bennett, Judy Gillispie, James Hershberger
Cover Design: James Hershberger
Cover Art: Steve Brown

Printed in China
First Edition 2021

1 2 3 4 5 6 7 8 9 10

062921

"Shut your eyes **TIGHT**!" Papa Bear said.
Clever Cub was so excited. He loved surprises!
What could it be? he wondered.
But when Papa Bear told him to open his eyes,
the surprise was better than anything he imagined!

"**BLACKBERRIES**!" Clever Cub shouted. "My favorite!"
Papa and Mama had led him to **BUNCHES** and **BUNCHES**
of blackberry bushes. Clever Cub jammed his face
into the soft, **SQUISHY** berries. He gobbled them up.

Mama Bear chuckled at Clever Cub's face.
"That's quite a purply ring around your mouth," she said.

"And quite a purply feeling in my **TUMMY**," the cub replied.
Clever Cub licked his mouth and thought hard.
"What was the best surprise you ever had, Papa?"

"I'll have to think about that," he replied.
"But I can tell you about *the* **BEST SURPRISE EVER**."

"I can't wait!" Clever Cub said as he kept eating berries.

"The story has a sad start," Papa Bear began.
"It was very early one morning long ago, just before dawn.
Two women walked toward a tomb."

"What's a *tomb*?" asked Clever Cub.

"It's a place where people are sometimes put after they die.
Back then, it was kind of like a small cave or room.
And a big, **BIG** stone was used to block the opening.
Their friend had died, and the women were going
to put good-smelling spices and oils on His body.
It's what people did then to care for friends who died."

Clever Cub looked sad. "Ohhh. That is sad.
Their friend must have been very special."

"He *was* special," Papa Bear said.
"He was **JESUS**, God's very own Son.
Jesus had come to earth to save people.
And it's sad and hard, but Jesus died on a cross
so that everyone could one day live with God."

10

Clever Cub scratched his nose.
It's what he did when he was thinking.
"So, Jesus gave up His whole life
to save everyone in the whole **WORLD**?"

"That's right, my clever cub," Mama Bear said.

"But on that third day, early in the morning, when the women were on their way, suddenly, the earth **QUAKED**!"

"**WOW**!" Clever Cub shouted. "What a surprise!"

Papa Bear nodded. "But there were bigger surprises to come."

"Bigger than an earthquake?" Clever Cub asked.

"**MUCH** bigger," Papa Bear said.

13

14

"Just as the earthquake struck,
an angel came down from heaven.
He rolled away the **BIG** stone in front of the tomb
and sat on it! The angel was **BRIGHT** as lightning.
His clothes were **WHITE** as snow. And when the guards
at the tomb saw the angel, they fainted and fell to the ground."

15

"**WOW**!" Clever Cub shouted again. "That *is* a bigger surprise. The best surprise ever!"

"Not quite," Papa Bear smiled.

"You mean there's **MORE**?" Clever Cub asked.

"Oh, yes! The angel told the women, 'Don't be scared.
I know that you have come to see Jesus,
but He is not here. For He has risen from the dead!'"

"What?" Clever Cub said.
And then he jumped up and
shouted louder than ever, "**WOW**!!"

Papa Bear continued. "The angel told the women
to go into the tomb and see for themselves.
And, sure enough, it was empty! Then the angel said,
'Tell this amazing news to Jesus' friends, the disciples.'

So off they ran, shaking with fear and joy and with their good news: 'Jesus has risen!' And guess what happened next!"

"A **BIGGER** earthquake?" Clever Cub said. "**MORE** angels?"

19

"No," Papa Bear chuckled. "Better than that. They ran straight into **JESUS**!"

"If I shout '**WOW**' any louder, I won't have any voice left!" Clever Cub said.

Clever Cub scratched his nose again as he thought.
"So Jesus was right there with the women,
just like you are here with me?"

"Just like that," Mama Bear nodded.

"And what did He say?" asked Clever Cub.

21

"He said, 'Hello!'" Papa Bear said with a grin. "Simple as that. And the women fell at His feet and worshipped Him. Then Jesus told them to tell His disciples to meet Him in Galilee. And off He went."

"And did Jesus meet them?" asked Clever Cub.

"Yes, and a lot **MORE!**" Papa Bear said.
"In fact, Jesus met with over five hundred people after He rose from the dead, just to make sure they knew He was really alive."

"And that's the **BEST SURPRISE EVER!**" Clever Cub shouted.

"Yes, indeed!" Papa Bear smiled.

For Clever Readers

Clever Cub is a curious little bear who **LOVES** to cuddle up with the Bible and learn about God! Clever Cub was so excited to hear about the **BEST SURPRISE EVER**, when Jesus rose from the dead! You can find the story in the Bible in Matthew 28:1–10.

What is the best surprise you ever had?

Clever Cub jumps when he is excited. What do you do when you are excited? Show how excited you are to know Jesus is alive!